Curious McCarthy's

Not-So-Perfect Pitch

by Tory Christie   illustrated by Mina Price

PICTURE WINDOW BOOKS
a capstone imprint

Curious McCarthy is published by Picture Window Books,
A Capstone Imprint
1710 Roe Crest Drive
North Mankato, Minnesota 56003
www.mycapstone.com

Text © 2018 Tory Christie
Illustrations © 2018 Picture Window Books

Cataloging-in-Publication Data is available on the Library of Congress website.
ISBN: 978-1-5158-1643-0 (library binding)
ISBN: 978-1-5158-1647-8 (paperback)
ISBN: 978-1-5158-1651-6 (eBook PDF)

Summary: After fourth-grade scientist Curious McCarthy observes her dad fixing their doorbell, she starts to wonder about the science of sound. Meanwhile at school, it's time for Curious to pick an instrument. Will she be stuck playing the clarinet like her three sisters?

Designer: Ashlee Suker

Printed and bound in Canada.
010382F17

For Nancy Brown — maybe you should
have encouraged me to play the flute.
And for Ms. Tibble — who knew
more about colds than kids.

DAD Engineer. Efficient, exact, precise.

MOM Highly sensible loser of keys.

CHARLOTTE (age 13) Clarinet squeaker. Toilet scrubber.

EMILY (age 12) She's weird.

MRS. STICKLER (age 103, I think) Fourth-grade teacher, ladybug lover, cowbell ringer.

MS. TIBBLE Music teacher offering great career advice.

MS. BROWN Band teacher and finder of keys.

MR. BUMBLE Orchestra teacher with an itchy case of dandruff.

ANNE (age 11) Future stand-up comic.

CURIOUS (age 10) Future scientist – not future musician.

The McCarthys

JOHN GLENN (age 8) Excellent burper of "The Star Spangled Banner."

BENJAMIN (age 5) A kindergartner with no sense of humor.

EDISON (age 4) The youngest McCarthy.

RANDY STUDLEY Excellent spitballer.

NADIA Mysterious character.

CARTER Even more mysterious character.

HENRY WONG Questionable spitballer.

LIN TRAN Part of the fourth-grade cold-lunch crowd at Hilltop Elementary.

ROBIN FINCH More of a warbler than a finch.

1

Sunday, 8:25 a.m.

The quieter you are, the more you are able to hear. At least that's what Mom always told me. And right now, I was quiet. I heard a mysterious noise. It sounded like a doorbell. The only problem was, it wasn't *our* doorbell.

DING-DONG.

I went to my bedroom door and looked down the hall.

DING-DONG.

I followed the sound down the back stairs.

DING-DONG.

I peeked into the kitchen, where I thought the noise was coming from.

DING-DONG.

There was no one in the kitchen. I walked into the living room.

There was Dad, his tools spread around him, lined up like little soldiers, ready for action.

"Hi," I said.

"Hi, Curious!" said Dad. "Do you want to help me finish putting in the new doorbell?"

"Why do we need a new doorbell?" I asked.

"The old one broke," he answered, stepping out the front door. "And I want it to chime in the kitchen."

That made sense because Dad spends about fifty percent of his time in the kitchen.[1]

Dad took out his tape measure to figure out how high to place the bell. He marked a spot on the front of the house, where he wanted the button to be.

"Isn't that a little high?" I asked.

---

1   This is a footnote. If you've read these books before, you know all about footnotes. If you haven't, scientists use footnotes to add important information. Here's that important information: Dad spends the other forty percent of his time sleeping. I know that doesn't equal one hundred percent, but you have to leave some time in the day for getting dressed or going to the bathroom or other things that I just don't want to think about.

"Yes, but the McCarthys are tall," said Dad.[2]

"The McCarthys don't ring their own doorbell," said my younger brother Ben.

Dad laughed. "I guess you're right, Ben."

----

2   Most doorbells are placed 122 centimeters from the floor. But Dad likes to place things higher.

Dad has projects every weekend. Last weekend he added a key rack behind the door. Here are some facts about Dad:

1. He rolls T-shirts when he's folding laundry.

2. His idea of a good time is reading a physics textbook.[3]

3. He is old.

4. He likes to cook.

5. He has a system for not losing his keys.

Actually, Dad has a system for everything.

DING-DONG.

Mom came down the stairs. "I really think the *DING* should move up an octave," she said.[4]

Mom was holding her choir music in one hand and putting on lipstick with the other. "Has anyone seen my keys?" she asked.

---

3   Physics is the study of matter and energy. You will learn all about that in high school. Don't worry about it for now. You have enough to worry about.

4   An octave is a series of eight notes. One octave higher would mean that the sound would be eight notes higher. It also means that it vibrates either twice or half as fast . . . I can never remember, but we will probably figure that out by the end of this book.

Here are some interesting facts about Mom:

1. She doesn't do laundry.

2. She reads books by dead people.

3. She is not as old as Dad, but she is two centimeters taller.

4. She hates to cook.

5. She loses her keys every day.

My three younger brothers and three older sisters scattered to search for the keys.

I stood still and observed.

I am good at observing. I checked my watch and recorded the time on my clipboard. Here are some interesting facts about me:

1. I am a scientist, and scientists don't do laundry.

2. My idea of a good time is doing anything other than reading.

3. I am older than exactly half of my siblings.

4. I like to *watch* Dad cook.

5. I don't have to worry about losing car keys at this stage of my life.

I watched as everyone searched. Ben looked under the couch. Emily opened the front closet. Anne checked a jacket pocket. Dad looked at the key rack.

Then Edison rechecked the couch. Charlotte rechecked the front closet. Ben checked the bookcase. Emily checked behind a chair. Anne checked the coffee table.

John Glenn wasn't checking or rechecking anything.

"FOUND THEM!" shouted John Glenn.

I looked at John Glenn suspiciously before I checked my clipboard. Then I checked my watch. It had been exactly 43 seconds.

John Glenn dangled the keys in front of Mom. He held out his right hand for his prize. Mom is known to hand out chocolate prizes.[5]

She ignored his hand and bent over and gave him a kiss. Then she rushed out the door for choir practice.

I didn't feel sorry for John Glenn. He probably hid the keys in the first place. Maybe Mom suspected that too. When he turned to go back to the kitchen, I made an interesting observation. He had a perfect lipstick smooch on his right cheek.

----

5   Or bribes. Like, to get us to stop embarrassing her at the store. There was one time when John Glenn burped "The Star Spangled Banner" at the grocery store. It is a scientific fact that you can't do that with chocolate in your mouth.

2

Sunday, 9:45 a.m.

I should probably introduce myself. My name is Curie McCarthy, but everyone calls me Curious. I am going to be a scientist when I grow up, so I try to practice a little each day. Sometimes scientists make lists. Here is a list of questions a scientist might ask:

1. Does chocolate taste good to porpoises?
2. Can you see Hawaii from outer space?
3. Can you feel an earthquake in North Dakota?
4. Why do dirty socks smell bad?
5. Can you hear your heartbeat when you're quiet?

I thought about what Mom was always saying. About how you can hear more when you are quiet.

And I decided that would be my hypothesis for this week.

Hypothesis:
The quieter you are,
the more you can hear.

A hypothesis is like a guess that hasn't been proven yet. I would spend the week observing and maybe even testing my hypothesis to prove that it is true.

With the doorbell installed, Dad piled us into the van. We headed off to church.

We walked into church and sat in the very middle. Dad says sitting in the middle helps us blend in. I'm not sure how that's possible.

Dad shuffled us around until he was convinced we were in the right order. The order that would cause the least fighting. The order that would cause the least fidgeting. The order that would keep us from standing out.

On this particular Sunday, we sat right behind my teacher, Mrs. Stickler. I was trying my best to keep from being noticed. And I was listening carefully.

I heard Mrs. Stickler clear her throat. Probably
getting ready to sing.

As the choir started, we stood up. I sang along
with the choir, but not too loudly. I wanted to hear
other voices. I watched the back of Mrs. Stickler's
dress. It was a crazy dress, with purple flowers and
small orange dots. Mrs. Stickler sang with gusto. Her
head swayed back and forth with the music.

I started swaying to the music too. I could hear Mom singing the alto part in the choir. I imagined her swaying up in the choir loft.

John Glenn suddenly burped during the refrain. Mrs. Stickler turned around and glared at me. *Great.*[6]

Mrs. Stickler probably thought I was the one who burped.

I observed my surroundings. Observing calms me down. I looked at Mrs. Stickler's dress. I saw one of the orange dots move.

It wasn't a dot — it was a ladybug. It started crawling up her back. John Glenn saw it too. He reached out a hand and was about to flick it. I grabbed his hand and pulled it back. He shook me off, and I fell back into Emily.[7]

Emily fell back onto the pew.

"OUCH!" Emily gasped.

---

6   This is not really great. This is called sarcasm. It is when you say something that you don't really mean. To have Mrs. Stickler think that I am the burper is NOT great.

7   Apparently, Dad did not get the order right!

Dad glanced over at us and gave us the look. The song ended. We all sat down. Mrs. Stickler glanced at me as she settled in to her spot.

I was going to have to find a way to get back at John Glenn. I looked over at him.

But then I realized I didn't have to get back at John Glenn. I saw the big lipstick smooch from Mom still on his cheek. I smiled.

3

Monday, 8:05 a.m.

The next day at school, Mrs. Stickler had an announcement.

"Class, in fifth grade you get to choose if you want to be in choir, band, or orchestra. You can only choose one. The choir is where you learn to sing as a group. But for band or orchestra, you'll need to choose an instrument. You might not get the instrument you want. That's because we don't need fifteen drummers and twenty-two tuba players," she said. "The music teachers and your parents will help you decide."

All three of my sisters play the clarinet. If I decided to play an instrument, I did not want to play the clarinet. I wanted to play something different.

I imagined the *OOOMPA* of a tuba drowning out their squeaky clarinets.

I snortled quietly.[8]

Mrs. Stickler glared at me. Apparently she has pretty good hearing.

I was sure that my parents would never agree to a tuba. That's all a family with seven kids would need around the house. It would take up too much space. It would cost too much money. It would make too much noise!

Mrs. Stickler explained all about our week. We'd learn about our three music options and all the different instruments we could play. Maybe being quiet this week and listening carefully would help me choose the right instrument.

"Your music teacher, Ms. Tibble, is coming to visit our class today. She will practice a song with us," Mrs. Stickler explained.

---

8   Snort + chortled = snortled. That's a word sandwich. It is a mix between choking and laughing. Kind of a pig-like sound that you make by mistake.

We would see what it was like to be in the choir. On Friday, we would have a concert. Mom would love it if I joined the choir.

"Tomorrow, the band and orchestra teachers are coming to talk with us," she continued.

"The band and orchestra are both groups of musicians that perform together. Each group features different kinds of instruments," she said. "But don't worry about that right now. We will explain it all in more detail later this week."

If we chose the band or orchestra, we would find out on Friday if we would get to play the instrument we wanted. Mrs. Stickler reminded us that we would not have fifteen drummers and twenty-two tuba players.[9]

Ms. Tibble walked into the room.

"Settle down, class," said Mrs. Stickler. "We have some fun things planned for today."

---

9   I could have told Mrs. Stickler that with only twenty-two kids in our class, her suggestion was mathematically impossible.

Ms. Tibble picked up a microphone and held it in front of her. She clicked the ON switch. "Does anyone know what this is?" she said into the microphone. It was really loud.

"A MICROPHONE!" several kids shouted. And I kind of perked up. A microphone can help people hear more — even if they aren't quiet. I wondered if this would be proof against my hypothesis. Maybe you don't have to be quiet to hear more — you can just get a microphone.

"Right," Ms. Tibble said. "Now this time I want you to raise your hand. Who would like to give it a try?"

I wanted a better look at that microphone. So I raised my hand.[10]

"Curious, come on up," Ms. Tibble called.

As I walked to the front of the room, I tried to think of a good joke.

----

10   Raising your hand might be a good strategy for some scientists, but not for me. Read on . . .

But when I got to the microphone, Ms. Tibble said, "Sing 'Happy Birthday' into the microphone, Curious."

I froze. She wanted me to *sing*? I looked over at Robin Finch. Robin is not my greatest pal. I saw her smirking at Nadia and Carter, who sat next to her.

I wasn't sure if I wanted to sing in front of everyone. Robin would probably start laughing.

But then I looked at Lin. She was smiling at me. That gave me the courage I needed.

I grabbed the microphone and started.

"Happy Birthday to you! Happy Birthday to . . ."

"STOP!" said Ms. Tibble. "Curious must have a cold," she announced to the class. "Her voice is a little froggy. That's what happens when you have a cold."

I nodded yes.[11]

I walked back to my seat. I had my head down. I did not want to look in Robin's direction.

----

11   For the record: I did not have a cold. That was my best voice.

24

This would go down in history as one of the
dumbest mistakes of the fourth grade. I thought again
of Mom's advice.

*The quieter you are, the more
you are able to hear.*

I should have listened to Mom.

Several other kids went up to the microphone to give it a try. They did not have colds.

At the end of the lesson, Ms. Tibble had us practice the song we would sing at Friday's concert. I just mouthed all the words. I didn't want anyone to hear my croaky voice.

I listened carefully as I pretended to sing. Lin was singing very softly . . . in Vietnamese. She looked at me and smiled.

Maybe that was proof of Mom's words — and my hypothesis. I wouldn't have heard Lin if I had been singing myself. I wondered what other interesting things I could hear by being quiet.

4

Monday, 1:15 p.m.

That afternoon, Mrs. Stickler marched us down to the library. But today she had the boys get in one line. Girls in another line. Mrs. Stickler is very old-fashioned. She marched because she's a Girl Scout. That's what Girl Scouts did in 1912.

We marched through the library doors. Mrs. Stickler left us with Mr. Grumpus, the librarian. Then she escaped to the teachers' lounge. She probably needed more coffee.

I snuck behind the bookshelves to the last row of nonfiction. This is where I like to spend some quiet time. I like to think of this as my laboratory.

I wanted to learn more about microphones. I also wanted to learn more about instruments.

I needed to know all about instruments so I could make the right choice. It was clear that I would not be singing in the choir.

I found a book about sensors. The cover of the book had a picture of a microphone. I wondered if sensors worked like our senses. I grabbed the book and moved on.[12]

I found the music books. I wasn't sure what instrument I wanted to play. I wasn't sure about a lot of things. I made a list of the things I wanted to know:

> 1. Does the height of the doorbell really matter?
> 2. How long do you have to play the clarinet before it stops squeaking?
> 3. How much louder is a flute than a tuba?
> 4. How much work does it take to get perfect pitch?[13]

12   We have five senses: taste, sight, touch, smell, and hearing. I needed to learn more about hearing and sound if I wanted to learn about music and microphones.
13   Pitch is the quality of a sound. Perfect pitch is the ability to sing a note exactly the right way. Obviously my pitch is less than perfect.

But then I remembered my Mom's words about being quiet in order to hear more.

As a scientist, I needed to continue to test my hypothesis. So, as I sat on the library floor, I listened.

I heard Randy, Nadia, and some other voices:

". . . my mom puts this stuff in my hair. It's called . . ."

". . . chicken à la king. But sometimes we have . . ."

". . . a booger, that's what. She had a booger hanging on her . . ."

". . . microphone when she croaked out . . ."

". . . a little froggy . . ."

I didn't hear anything more. I was thinking about my froggy voice.

And that is why I did not hear the footsteps. Lin had walked up behind me. She was quiet too.

I wondered if she heard the kids talking about my

froggy voice.

She smiled at me and showed me her books. She

had a book called *The Cricket in Times Square*.[14]

----

14   This is a book by George Selden. It is a classic. Mom has read it to the boys and
me. Crickets make music with their wings. They rub them together kind of like a violin.

Her second book was *Frog and Toad Are Friends.*[15]

We walked to the checkout counter together. I checked out *How Sensors Work.* My second book was called *Musical Instruments for the Curious Kid.*

---

15   This is a chapter book by Arnold Lobel. It was one of my favorites in second grade. I chose to focus on the "friend" part of the title and not the "frog" part.

Monday, 4:35 p.m.

"You should really play the clarinet," Emily said.

Dad nodded.

"But I think I might like the flute," I said. "Or the tuba," I whispered.

I saw Mom and Dad exchange a look. I did not know what the look meant, but I knew it wasn't good.

Dad started explaining about the clarinet. "It has the widest range in pitch of all instruments," he said.

Mom was quiet.

All three of my sisters play the clarinet. Emily decided that next year she would switch to the bassoon. It also meant we would have an extra clarinet. My parents were probably thinking about the extra cost of a flute . . . or tuba.

Why would a flute cost more than a clarinet?
A flute is smaller, so it should cost less. But a tuba
was *way* bigger. It would probably cost a fortune.

I peered out the kitchen door to the back porch.
Charlotte was there, practicing her clarinet. Actually,
she was licking the reed and not playing at all.[16]

"Why do you do that?" I asked.

----
16   A reed is a strip of wood that vibrates. It gets stuck to the mouthpiece of the
clarinet. It helps produce the sound . . . or squeak.

"You have to keep the reed wet so that it vibrates properly," she answered.

Properly . . . Charlotte did *everything* properly.

"That's gross," I said. I knew that I was not going to play the clarinet. No licking reeds for me. I just had to figure out how to convince my family.

6

Monday, 6:00 p.m.

That night at dinner, we all dashed around the dinner table.

Dinner was another chance for me to test my hypothesis. I was going to be extra quiet so I could hear more. Listening is a very good skill for a scientist.

Listening is also a good skill for an eater. Some scientists study animal senses. Some animals have to use their hearing to find dinner. Wolves can hear the sound of their prey up to ten kilometers away. Sharks are good at hearing the low frequencies of wounded fish.[17]

---

17 Frequencies tell how fast sound waves are vibrating. Low frequencies mean slow vibrations and deeper sounds. Dad's voice has a lower frequency than Mom's. But he's not wounded . . . at least I don't think he is.

The boys were shoving and pushing. They tried to get a good seat at the far end of the table. Dad brought out his famous black bean hot dish.[18]

"What did one eye say to the other?" Anne asked.

"Eyes don't talk," answered Ben.

"Between you and me, something smells!" Anne laughed.

"Why did the chicken cross the road?" asked John Glenn. He is not very good at jokes, so I was curious. I wanted to hear the answer.

"To get away from the clarinet recital!" John Glenn laughed.

Anne said, "Why did the clarinet player get arrested?"

No one said anything.

"She got in treble!" Anne laughed.

"I don't get it," said Ben.

---

18 A hot dish is a casserole. It contains all the leftovers from the week before plus a can of green beans. Then it is topped with tater tots and heated in the oven. A hot dish can be good . . . sometimes.

As we passed our plates around, John Glenn started making puking sounds. Charlotte's lips were pursed. It looked like she was getting ready to squeak her clarinet.

But she said, "Yum! Black bean hot dish. My favorite!"

Emily said, "Curious, you can have my clarinet. Then I can start playing the bassoon!"

"What if I play the flute?" I asked. Mom smiled at me. I think she realized that I did not want to play the clarinet.

"You have to play the clarinet, Curious!" said Anne. "Then we can share music."

"But the flute sounds better than the clarinet," I said.

Charlotte glared at me. I stopped talking. I couldn't test my hypothesis if I was talking.

"Did you hear my last practice session?" Charlotte turned and asked Mom.

"I sure hope it was your last," John Glenn muttered under his breath. But no one else heard him.

"Yes, you are getting so good, Charlotte," Mom said. Mom has good hearing. So I was pretty sure that she heard all the squeaking. I just wasn't sure why she hadn't mentioned it.

"Curious, I can show you how to place your fingers over the holes. That is how you make the different notes," Charlotte said. But the thought of putting my mouth on that clarinet sent shivers down my spine. Didn't these people know about germs? As a scientist, I knew all about germs.

7

Monday, 7:52 p.m.

That night Mom read to us. She read *Sarah, Plain and Tall*. She read in the boys' room, because Edison would always fall asleep before the end.

I wondered if this Sarah Plain lady was as tall as the McCarthys. I wondered if she ever thought about the height of her doorbell.

I thought the book was interesting. But John Glenn didn't like it. He was hanging upside down over Ben's bunk. In the middle of reading a sentence, Mom stopped. She said, "John Glenn, stay on your own bunk." And then she continued to read.

She never moved her eyes from the book. How did she know what John Glenn was doing? It really made me wonder about her super-sensing ability.

Was she listening at the same time that she was reading? Did she hear John Glenn's bed springs squeaking as he dangled over the side?

But if that was true, she didn't have to be quiet to hear more. That was some evidence against my hypothesis — apparently moms hear more even if they aren't quiet. Or my hypothesis doesn't apply to moms.

8

Tuesday, 10:04 a.m.

Mrs. Stickler reminded us again that the choir was for singers. She gave me a strange look.

"Our middle school band has woodwind, brass, and percussion instruments," she said. "The orchestra has string instruments."

To help us choose the right instrument, we would talk to the choir, band, and orchestra teachers. These are called interviews.[19]

Mrs. Stickler sent us out of the room in three lines. This worked out perfectly because one student was absent that day. With twenty-one kids, there were seven kids in each line.

---

19   An interview is usually a face-to-face meeting. It includes lots of questions and answers. Interviews are used to get information. Sometimes, an interviewer will try to trick an interviewee. Like a police officer trying to get a criminal to confess. Or a parent trying to get you to tattle on your little brother. But nothing like that has ever happened to me. Honest.

We marched down the hall. We stood outside the music room. Every six minutes, three kids were called in. They would get a chance to talk with Ms. Tibble; Ms. Brown, who was the band teacher; and Mr. Bumble, the orchestra teacher. When they were done, they were sent down to the lunchroom.

Now if Dad was running this show, he would see how inefficient this was. He would come up with a better system. Why have all these kids standing in line doing nothing? They could be reading. Or doing math. Or sharpening pencils.

I stood in line behind Lin. Robin was at the end of the second line. Randy Studley was at the end of the third line.

Then it was just three of us left. Robin said, "I am not going to play an instrument. I am going to sing in the choir. My mother says I have a lovely voice. A *lovely* voice."

9

Tuesday, 11:07 a.m.[20]

Ms. Tibble called me over to her desk.

"How would you like to be in the choir, Curious?" she asked.

"Actually, I would like to play an instrument," I said. She seemed relieved.

Next I was sent to Mr. Bumble, the orchestra teacher.

Mr. Bumble introduced himself. He scratched his messy hair and smiled. But I was distracted. Ms. Brown, the band teacher, was looking at me. She smiled too.

"Is your whole family as tall as you are?" Mr. Bumble asked.

---

20   Have you been keeping track of the time? Have you noticed how much time we've wasted? That is why we need a better system.

"No," I said. "My little brothers are shorter than me."

"I mean, are your parents tall?" he said.

"Yes," I answered. I was beginning to doubt Mr. Bumble's interviewing skills. I glanced over at Ms. Brown. She was still looking at me. Her smile twisted as she scribbled something in her notebook.

I turned back to Mr. Bumble. "I want to play the flute," I said. His smile disappeared.

"You should really think about the bass fiddle. It's a fine instrument. You're nice and tall. Bass players need to be tall," he said.

I guess the teachers had to find kids to play all the different instruments. But I didn't want to get stuck playing the bass . . . or the clarinet.

He went on for a minute about how great the bass was. Then he said, "You can rent a bass from school. How does that sound?"

"Great," I mumbled.

"Just think about it and talk it over with your parents," he said.

Then we switched again. I went over to talk to Ms. Brown.

"I want to play the flute," I said right away, so we could just get to the point.

"Oh, we have a lot of flute players," she said. "And your lips aren't quite right to play the flute."

When she said it, Robin and Randy turned and looked over at me. Oh, *great*.[21]

"Let's see," Ms. Brown said. "Pucker your lips — as if you were going to kiss someone."

I just stared at her. I could hear Randy and Robin giggling.

"Come on," she said. "Pucker!"

I put my lips together. It wasn't really a pucker. I heard more giggles from across the room.

---

21   This is sarcasm again. Obviously, it was NOT great that Robin and Randy overheard Ms. Brown's opinion of my lips. It was awful. And just what was wrong with my lips anyway?

"That's not going to work," she said. "Let's try something else. Pretend you are spitting out a watermelon seed."

Ms. Brown must be batty. Spitting is not allowed in school. "Come on," she said. "Spit out that watermelon seed. I need to see your embouchure."[22]

----

22   That word is pronounced, "OM-boo-shur." I am pretty smart. But I had no idea what that meant.

Ms. Brown was scaring me. She waited. She stared. I stared back.

"You know, the band has brass and percussion instruments too," she said.

"I know," I said. "But Mrs. Stickler said that we don't need fifteen drummers and twenty-two tuba players."

Ms. Brown laughed. "Well, we do have a lot of drummers, but no one has signed up to play the tuba yet. And it helps to be tall to play the tuba."

I smiled. Maybe I could tell that to my parents.

The bell rang. Randy, Robin, and I were dismissed. We walked to lunch.

"Look!" Randy laughed. "I can spit out a watermelon seed!" He pretended to spit.

Robin made smoochy noises with her lips. She laughed too.

I was just glad I got out of that room without having to show anyone my embouchure.

My worries weren't completely over, though. What would my parents say about the tuba?

And would my sisters be mad? Where would we store it? How would I get it home? Maybe it would be easier to convince them that I should play the flute.

10

Tuesday, 3:46 p.m.

I walked in after school, following Anne. She was carrying her clarinet case. It was nice and small. I wondered how I would carry a tuba. Maybe tuba cases had wheels. But a flute case could fit in my backpack. And a flute is quieter. Maybe I should pick the flute.

"How was school?" asked Dad.

"Great!" said Anne.

"Fine," I said softly. Mom looked my way. She seemed concerned.

"We read books," said Ben.

"We got to make slime!" shouted John Glenn.[23]

----

23   Lucky second graders. Teachers should realize that it is just as educational for fourth graders to make slime. We need to use all of our senses, including our sense of touch. Research has shown that playing with messy substances improves fine motor skills. And if kids laugh in the process, this increases blood flow to the brain. If your teachers don't let you make slime, you should check out my book, *Curious McCarthy's Power of Observation* for a slime recipe. Just don't mention that I told you.

Tuesday, 6:00 p.m.

As we shoved around the table for Taco Tuesday, John Glenn was still talking about his slime. Everyone seemed to be talking. I stayed quiet. I really wondered if I would be able to hear more. I had my clipboard with me to record some observations.

"May I have some tomatoes, please?" asked Charlotte.

"Pass the lettuce, POR FAVOR!" said Emily.[24]

As Anne started telling another joke, I heard the doorbell. I looked around. No one else appeared to have heard it. Maybe Mom was right about hearing more when you are quiet. More evidence that my hypothesis was correct. I wrote that down on my clipboard.

DING-DONG.

This time Charlotte looked up. She heard the doorbell too.

---

24 *Por favor* means *please* in Spanish. Emily is a very polite weird person.

"I'll get it," she said and walked out of the room.

"Please pass the cheese," said Ben.

"Please cut the cheese!" John Glenn laughed.

"Me too," said Edison.

Charlotte walked back into the room.

"Mom," she said, "it's Ms. Brown."

I was startled. Why was Ms. Brown at my house? Mom got up from the table and walked to the front door.

I imagined Ms. Brown talking to Mom about my embouchure. I listened hard, trying to hear what they were saying. I heard them laugh. My heart thumped. I could feel my face getting hot. Were they laughing about me?

Mom came back into the room. I studied her face, but she didn't look my way.

"Ms. Brown brought my keys back," she said. "I left them in the choir loft on Sunday."

"Quick!" said Dad, "Put them on the key rack before they get lost again."

Tuesday, 7:47 p.m.

That night, Mom continued to read *Sarah, Plain and Tall*. I listened carefully. Sarah must have been really tall if it was important enough to put it in the title. I wondered if she was tall enough to play the bass fiddle . . . or the tuba.[25]

---

25 *Sarah, Plain and Tall* is historical fiction. It takes place before school buses were invented. That means Sarah didn't have to worry about taking her fiddle or her tuba on the bus. Lucky Sarah.

11

Wednesday, 8:05 a.m.

I walked into Mrs. Stickler's class. Ms. Brown was there for some reason.

"Hi, Curious," she said to me. "Did your mom find her keys this morning?"

"I think so," I answered.

"Let's get settled, class," said Mrs. Stickler. "We have some fun planned for this morning."

I turned and walked to my desk.

"Ms. Brown has brought some musical instruments," said Mrs. Stickler. "I want you to put on your listening ears and focus your attention on Ms. Brown."[26]

----

26   The ear is a very complex sensor. The part of the ear that is on the outside of your head is a sound collector. The real hearing is done with a bunch of bones inside your skull. I thought about looking in my desk for another set of "listening" ears, but I didn't think Mrs. Stickler would think that was funny.

"Listening is an important skill for musicians," said Ms. Brown. "Many musicians listen to recordings. Sometimes they try to mimic other musicians. That helps them play better. Today we are going to talk about the woodwind family," said Ms. Brown. "Let's start with the smallest. This is a piccolo."

She picked up a very tiny flute. She puckered her lips and blew into it. I wondered if this was the mysterious embouchure. I used my listening ears. It sounded very high pitched.

I thought I might play the piccolo. It would fit inside my backpack. My parents would like that. But it might remind me of Robin Finch.[27]

Ms. Brown continued. She picked up the flute and played it.

Then she picked up the clarinet. "Now class, this is the most beautiful sounding instrument."

----

27   Robin may have perfect pitch, but her voice is a little like scratching a chalkboard. And since you probably don't have chalkboards in your school, you should ask an old person what that sounds like.

I was suspicious. Was that what she came to talk to Mom about last night? Was she trying to convince her that I should play the clarinet? Then why did she even mention the tuba to me? I'll bet Mom's lost keys were just a trick. All part of her plan. She reminded me of John Glenn when he "found" Mom's keys.

Ms. Brown licked the reed. She pursed her lips. Then she played the clarinet. She didn't even squeak once. It was very nice. Nothing like my sisters.

Ms. Brown explained the other woodwinds.

This seems like another good place for a list. This is the woodwind family:

Woodwinds

1. Piccolo
2. Flute
3. Clarinet
4. Alto saxophone
5. Bassoon
6. English horn
7. Oboe

Ms. Brown played the rest of the woodwinds. But my listening ears were off. I was mad that Mom and Ms. Brown were plotting against me. I bet they were going to make me play the clarinet.

When Ms. Brown was finished, Mrs. Stickler had us practice singing a song for Friday night's concert. Our music teacher, Ms. Tibble, wasn't there because we shared her with Eastwood Elementary.[28]

I just mouthed the words again. I did not want anyone to hear my not-so-perfect pitch.

---

28   Eastwood is a school that is *west* of Hilltop. And is nowhere near the woods. It is surrounded by prairie. You've got to wonder who is in charge of naming schools around here.

12

Wednesday, 6:31 p.m.

Wednesday night is chore night for the McCarthys. It also means choir practice for Mom.

I was at the table folding towels.

"Has anyone seen my keys?" Mom asked.

I looked at John Glenn. Dad had him standing on a chair scrubbing pots and pans. I observed a mountain of bubbles coming from the sink.

"Check the key rack," said Dad.

"I'll go look," I said. I would do almost anything to get out of folding towels. Folding towels is a job fit for Charlotte. She's better at tight corners and perfect squares.

But I wasn't going to trade chores — Charlotte was scrubbing the toilet.

I walked past Ben. He was sweeping the kitchen floor. Edison was sorting spoons and forks. Anne was carrying another load of laundry to the table. Emily was vacuuming the plushy shag carpet in the living room.

I walked to the key rack. No keys.

"Not here!" I shouted to Mom. She didn't answer. I walked back to the kitchen, but she wasn't there. John Glenn was snooping at the back door. A trail of bubbles followed him across the floor. I walked over to see who he was spying on. Mom and Dad were on the back porch.

". . . that's what Nancy Brown said," Mom was saying to Dad.

"Are you sure?" asked Dad.

"Well, I can talk to her tonight at choir practice," Mom said.

Nancy Brown? As in *Ms. Brown*? Were Mom and Ms. Brown friends?

I wondered what Mom was going to talk to her about. My embouchure? The clarinet?

Before stepping off the porch, Mom gave Dad a big smooch. She was probably warming up her embouchure.

I went back to my towels.

"Knock-knock," said Anne.

"Who's there?" said Edison, Ben, and John Glenn all at the same time.[29]

"Figs," said Anne.

"Figs who?" we asked.[30]

"Figs the doorbell. It's broken," said Anne.

"Again?" asked Dad as he walked in through the back door.

---

29   This caught my attention. It reminded me of how sensors work. Sensors send a signal to get a response. Anne said two words (a signal) and got three brothers to respond with two words (response). Parents and teachers might want to pay attention to this.

30   And this was also a signal and a response, but in this case it was a completely new word. Some scientists call this echo-response. All kids know how knock-knock jokes work, but I wondered if they understood the relation to sensors. I also wondered why they don't do DING-DONG jokes instead of KNOCK-KNOCK jokes. This is the twenty-first century after all.

13

Thursday, 8:07 a.m.

Mrs. Stickler rang a cowbell. Everyone snapped to attention and looked to the front of the room. She doesn't usually use a cowbell. She usually shouts, "Zip the lips!"[31]

Mrs. Stickler seemed a little alarmed that we all reacted so quickly. After a pause, she said, "Both Ms. Brown and Mr. Bumble are going to talk to us today! Aren't we lucky? They are going to talk about more musical instruments. Please line up and we will walk quietly to the music room."

When we got to the music room, Ms. Brown announced, "Today we are going to talk about the percussion family."

---

31   About forty percent of new teachers don't make it through the first year. I think they get frustrated with kids who won't listen. Maybe they need cowbells.

She scanned the music room. When she got to me, her smile widened. Weird.

"And the string family!" interrupted Mr. Bumble.

"Who would like to try a drum?" Ms. Brown asked. After Monday's microphone experiment, no way was I going to raise my hand. A drum seems pretty easy, but she might make us sing along.

Lin raised her hand high. Then everyone else in the class raised their hands. Everyone, that is, except me. As Ms. Brown was assigning drums and bells, I observed. Here is the list of percussion instruments that were in the room:

Percussion

1. Snare drum
2. Cymbals
3. Triangle
4. Tambourine
5. Timpani
6. Xylophone
7. Piano
8. Bass drum
9. Bongo drums
10. Maracas

"Curious, would you like to give the bass fiddle a try?" asked Mr. Bumble. The bass looked like it might topple right on top of Mr. Bumble. It was ginormous.[32]

"No, thanks," I replied.

"I'll try!" said Nadia. She is not very tall. I wondered if she could even hold the thing.

These were the string instruments in the room:

Strings

1. Violin
2. Viola
3. Cello
4. Bass fiddle
5. Harp

"As you can see," said Ms. Brown, "there are a lot more instruments in the percussion family than in the string family."

She glanced competitively at Mr. Bumble.

He scratched his head.

----

32 Ginormous is a word sandwich that combines gigantic and enormous. That means HUGE, in case you haven't figured it out.

"With small families, you get more personal attention," said Mr. Bumble after a pause.[33]

Randy, Robin, and Henry couldn't resist giving little taps or shakes to their instruments. Lin tapped the drum. Nadia plucked the bass fiddle. Some of the other kids were talking excitedly about their instruments. Everyone was making noise.

Mrs. Stickler rang her cowbell. *REALLY LOUD.* Everyone was quiet. We looked at Mrs. Stickler.[34]

"We have a lot of chatterboxes in this class," Mrs. Stickler said.

"Actually," said Ms. Brown, "A chatterbox can be a type of percussion instrument." Mr. Bumble and Ms. Brown seemed to enjoy all the noise and confusion.

Robin leaned my way.

"My mother calls me a chatterbox sometimes," she said. "That means I am socially gifted."

----

33   He's got that right. In a family of nine, you get very little attention.
34   This signal and response business really works. My parents should probably get a cowbell – or a cymbal.

I thought, *The quieter you are, the more you are able to hear.*

"My mother also says I have perfect pitch," said Robin.

Mr. Bumble and Ms. Brown finished explaining the instruments. Everyone was given a chance to try one.

I looked over at the corner of the room and saw a tuba. We weren't learning about the brass instruments today, so I doubted the teachers would let me try it. And I certainly didn't want to make a fool of myself again in front of the whole class.

Ms. Brown walked over to me. "Would you like to try the tuba, Curious?"

I did want to try the tuba. And since everyone else was making so much noise, it probably would be safe. I nodded yes.

Ms. Brown de-germed the mouthpiece. Then she handed me the tuba. I wobbled. She put out her hands. I think she expected me to fall.

I blew into it. Nothing but air.

"Smile a little before you put the mouthpiece to your mouth," said Ms. Brown, "and buzz your lips together as you blow." She showed me what she meant by making a buzzing noise through her pinched lips.

Smiling was better than spitting a watermelon seed or smooching. So I smiled.

"Now take a deep breath," she said. I took the deepest breath that I could. I didn't wait for her to finish. I blew hard.

TWOOOoooOOOoooMPAHHHHH!

The entire class looked my way.

Mrs. Stickler staggered back into the door.

The clock fell off the wall.

Ms. Brown cheered. "I've never heard a fourth grader blow a tuba that loudly!"

I looked around. Everyone was smiling at me. At that moment, I knew that the tuba was the right instrument for me.

Next we practiced our song for the concert. And by "we," I do not mean me. I just mouthed the words again. I would keep my not-so-perfect pitch to myself. And besides, I had to save my energy. My brain was working hard trying to figure out a way to convince my parents that I had to play the tuba.

14

Thursday, 4:01 p.m.

"Time for clarinet practice," Charlotte said. Emily and Anne grabbed their clarinets. They followed Charlotte into the living room.

"You might want to practice outside," Dad said. "The clarinet sounds better outside."

I doubted this, but my sisters turned and walked out the back door.

As their squeaking began, I imagined myself playing the tuba with them. If the clarinet sounds better outside, the tuba would probably sound boomerocious.[35]

The boys and I helped Dad with dinner. We were having another one of his hot dishes.

----

35 Boomerocious is not a real word. But it should be.

"Curious, you can brown the meat," said Dad.
I looked at him suspiciously. I wondered if that was
a reference to Ms. Brown.

I took the pan from him and listened. The meat
began to *sizzle* in the pan. I listened to Dad *chop-
chop* the onions.

I listened to John Glenn *bang* the cans of green
beans together. Ben was opening and closing the
fridge with a *FWAP-FWAP*. Edison was *tapping* the
table with wooden spoons. It seemed like we had our
own percussion family . . . and we were accompanied
by the distant squeaking of clarinets.

Thursday, 6:00 p.m.

We crowded around the table.

"We need some new reeds," said Charlotte as we dished out hot dish.

"We just bought reeds last week," said Mom.

"Yeah, but we've all been practicing a lot," said Charlotte. "Some of the reeds chipped."

"Reeds are expensive," said Mom. "Maybe you girls could be more careful."

"Flutes don't need reeds," I said quietly.

Neither do tubas, I thought. I imagined how shocked my sisters would be if I brought home a tuba. I started to laugh and choked on a noodle. Mom gave me a worried look.

"Maybe I can fix the reeds," said Dad. Anne rolled her eyes.

"No ES POE-SEE-BLAY!" said Emily.[36]

"I used to be a pretty good whittler way back when," Dad continued.

I took a bite of a pickle. I happen to love pickles, but the sourness made me pucker. I wondered if pickle eating was a good way to practice your embouchure.

---

36   Emily was trying to say the Spanish version of "it's not possible." I think.

The doorbell rang. Mom went to answer it.

"Knock-knock," said Anne.

"Who's there?" answered about half the family. Not me, because I was trying to listen to Mom. She was talking to someone at the front door. And also because I had a pickle in my mouth.

"Justin," said Anne.

"Justin who?" asked John Glenn, Ben, and Edison.

"Justin time for dinner!" shouted Anne.

As my brothers and sisters chatted away, I was quiet. I tried to ignore the noise so that I could hear who Mom was talking to.[37]

And I thought about my hypothesis. What if I was quiet, but no one else was quiet? Then even if I was quiet, I wouldn't be able to hear. Maybe my hypothesis was not very good. I tried really hard to hear Mom through all the chatter.

----

37   Noise is an unwanted sound. Scientists think of noise like background chatter. It gets in the way of the signal that you are trying to hear. In this case I was trying to hear Mom's voice (the signal) and didn't want to hear the chatter of my siblings (the noise). Did you know that noise is from the Latin word *nausea*? That means *puke*.

". . . we will think about it," I heard Mom saying.

She walked back into the kitchen just in time
to hear Anne's next joke. But she wasn't looking at
Anne, she was looking at me.

"Knock-knock!" said Anne.

"Who's there?" we asked.

"Impatient cow," said Anne.

"Impatient c—"

"MOO!" shouted Anne.[38]

Everybody cracked up except Ben and Edison.
They didn't get it.

---

38   Cows are generally quiet animals. But they do tend to make noise when they are
hungry – kind of like my little brothers.

16

Friday, 1:26 p.m.

The next day in school, Randy and Henry had taken straws from the lunchroom and were wadding up paper. They made spitballs and blew them through the straws. I watched as they wrapped their lips tightly around the straws. *FTEWP.* Randy tried to hit the windows at the side of the room. Henry noticed me looking at them.

"You like my embouchure, Curious?" Henry asked. Randy must have told him about my interview. I ignored him.

Mrs. Stickler tapped a pencil on her desk. She was trying to get our attention. It did not work, so she stood up and walked to the board.[39]

---

39   I should probably explain to Mrs. Stickler that a signal only works if it is unique. Rapping her pencil and using her voice are never going to work on this class. She should go back to the cowbell.

Ms. Brown was at the front of the room next to Mrs. Stickler. She picked up a trumpet and blew into it loudly. That worked. Our heads snapped to face the front of the room. Ms. Brown smiled. Mrs. Stickler looked alarmed.

"Today I am going to show you the instruments in the brass family," said Ms. Brown. "We already heard one of these instruments yesterday," she said as she smiled at me. "And today you'll get to hear the rest of the brass instruments," she continued.

This is another good place for a list. These are the instruments in the brass family:

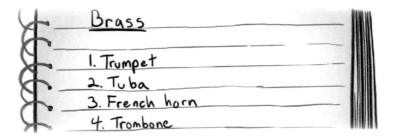

Brass

1. Trumpet
2. Tuba
3. French horn
4. Trombone

Ms. Brown started with the trumpet. She played a few notes and talked about lip vibration.

"Sometimes it tickles," she said. Henry was behind me making smooching sounds. I still ignored him.

Next she picked up the tuba.

She played a few really deep notes. Then smiled in my direction. I was pretty sure that Randy was doing something behind me. Something that was getting Ms. Brown's attention. I didn't turn around.

Next Ms. Brown picked up the French horn.

Finally, Ms. Brown played the trombone. She explained how trombones use a slide to change the sound that comes out of them. This is called its pitch. When the trombone is lengthened with the slide, the pitch is lowered.

"But listen to this!" Ms. Brown said excitedly.

She pulled a plunger out of her bag. Yes, a *toilet* plunger! I wondered what she was going to do with it. Mrs. Stickler continued to look alarmed.

"Don't worry, it's new," Ms. Brown said. "It has never been inside a toilet. You can buy plungers at the music store, but they are more expensive. I go to the hardware store for mine!"

She took the rubber part of the plunger and held it to the horn end of the trombone.

"*WAH-wah-WAH-WAH-waaaaahhhh,*" said the trombone.

Just like Charlie Brown's teacher in the Peanuts movies. I wondered if Charlie Brown was related to Ms. Brown.[40]

I listened to the *WAH-wah-WAH* with interest. I wondered if that is how Mrs. Stickler's voice sounded to Henry and Randy — just background chatter for those who never paid attention.

After Ms. Brown finished with the trombone, she packed up her things.

Mrs. Stickler had us sing our concert song. "This is your last chance to practice before the concert tonight," she said.

"Don't forget to invite your parents," added Ms. Brown. She smiled in my direction again. But there was no way I was going to turn around. I didn't want Randy or Henry to catch me looking at them again.

----

40   You must know the Peanuts TV specials: *A Charlie Brown Christmas* and *It's the Great Pumpkin, Charlie Brown*. Lucy, Linus, Snoopy, and the rest of the Peanuts characters were created by a guy named Charles Schulz in 1950. If you don't know about Peanuts, ask your parents . . . or grandparents . . . or somebody really old.

17

Friday, 5:13 p.m.

Because of the concert, we had dinner early. Dad does not do well with schedule changes. He skipped the homemade pizza that we usually have on Fridays. He made pizza burgers instead.[41]

DING-DONG.

"Curious, can you get that?" asked Dad.

I went to the front door. But there was no one there. I walked back to the kitchen.

"Who was it?" asked Dad.

"There was no one there," I said.

DING-DONG.

I looked at Dad. He shrugged his shoulders.

---

41   This is a very economical type of pizza. Tomato sauce and leftover meat on top of day-old hamburger buns. I was pretty sure that he included some leftover hot dish too.

"Could someone get that? I am trying to study," shouted Charlotte.

I walked back to the front door. Still no one there.

I went back to the kitchen just as John Glenn walked in from the backyard. He was laughing.

"Knock-knock," he said.

"Do you mean *DING-DONG*?" I asked.

"Yeah, *DING-DONG*," he said, laughing.

"Who's there?" I asked.[42]

"Irene," said Anne, who didn't miss a beat as she walked into the kitchen.

"Irene who?" John Glenn and I asked.

"Irene and Irene and no one comes to the door!" laughed Anne.

---

42   I was trying to think like a scientist. I started to see the knock-knock joke as a formula. It has a standard message and a standard response. Scientists use formulas all the time. But I also was trying to catch John Glenn off guard to see if this nonstandard *DING-DONG* would work.

18

Friday, 7:01 p.m.

"To start out the evening . . . ," began Ms. Tibble.
She tapped the microphone. She waited for the
audience to quiet down. Then she said, "Our fourth
graders will sing a song."

I stood in the back row of the risers. I peered over
Henry's head and saw my family in the bleachers.[43]

"Do-Re-Mi-Fa-Sol-La-Ti-Do!" sang Ms. Tibble. She
was giving us the right pitch.[44]

She raised her baton in the air. She held it there
for a few seconds. We waited. Then she quickly
brought the baton down for the first beat. We sang,
"Doe, a deer, a female deer . . ."

----

43   I was at the top of the risers, which is behind everyone else. My family was at the
top of the bleachers. The tall people always get stuck in back.
44   Studying music is like studying a new language. If you don't understand Ms.
Tibble, don't worry. I don't understand her all the time either.

And when I say "we," I don't mean me. *I* mouthed
the words and listened to the rest of the class sing.
And Ms. Tibble was mouthing the words too — in an
exaggerated way. She kind of reminded me of Emily
when she was trying to speak Spanish.

I glanced at the audience. Mom was smiling and
nodding her head. I looked around and saw Robin
glaring at me. So I exaggerated my mouth movements.

When the song was over, Ms. Tibble handed each of us an envelope. Then we joined our families in the bleachers. Robin's mother was sitting near my family. I heard Robin's mother say, "You have such a lovely voice, Robin. Perfect pitch!" Robin glanced my way and smirked.

Next, we listened to the fifth-grade band. I looked at the envelope. It said:

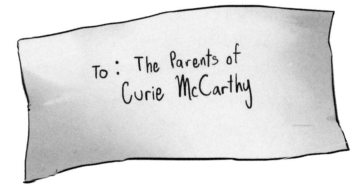

To: The Parents of
Curie McCarthy

"Listen to the clarinets," whispered Charlotte to Emily and me. "A clarinet can play four octaves."[45]

---

45   Remember in the first chapter I said we would talk more about octaves? An octave is a series of eight notes. When your music teacher sings, "Do-Re-Mi-Fa-Sol-La-Ti-Do," that is an octave. The second "Do" has twice the frequency as the first "Do." Frequency is the rate that the sound waves move.

The song ended. Except for a loud SQUEAK. We all looked toward Anne, who was sitting in the second row of the band. She was glancing up at us, her face red.

Then suddenly John Glenn let out a big burp. All attention turned to him. Now *Mom's* face was red. She bent her head and started rummaging in her giant purse. She handed the boys chocolate kisses and told them to keep quiet.

The band left the stage. As the orchestra settled in, Anne made her way up the bleachers.

Mr. Bumble kept smiling in our direction as he introduced the orchestra.

"Now, ladies and gentlemen," said Mr. Bumble, "we have the strings. Fourth-grade parents should pay attention to how the string and bow together help hand-eye coordination. Children who play in the orchestra become high achievers. Albert Einstein rarely left home without his violin."

And with that, the orchestra played.

After the concert, most of the families made a mad dash to Bridgeman's Ice Cream Shop across the street. But not the McCarthys.

Ice cream for a family with seven kids costs about as much as a trip to Disneyland. My parents would have had to work that into the budget three years ago. So Mom and Dad took their time getting ready to go.

I handed Mom the envelope.

"What did you think of the band, Curious?" Mom asked me.

"Fantastical," I said without much excitement.[46]

She started opening the envelope. I tried to peek over her shoulder.

I saw Ms. Brown heading our way. She had Mom and Dad in her sights. Mr. Bumble was on the other side of the gym. He dodged two trombones and a cello trying to work his way to the bleachers too.

----
46   *Fantastical* is a *real* word that basically means the band was fantastic, but in a fancy way. I don't know if it is a word sandwich, but it probably should be: fantastic + musical = fantastical.

"Mr. and Mrs. McCarthy," Mr. Bumble said, reaching us first. Mom and Dad had just reached the bottom of the bleachers. "I wanted to tell you about the scholarship possibilities for kids who play the bass fiddle."[47]

"Scholarships?" Dad perked up at those words.

"Yes," answered Mr. Bumble. "There are so many clarinet players that those scholarships are harder to get." He glanced sadly at my sisters.

Ms. Brown was heading in our direction. Mom smiled and greeted her.

"I don't think we'll need to worry about scholarships," Mom said, shoving the envelope into her purse.

"We won't?" said Dad, Charlotte, Emily, and Anne all together.

"Well not for Curious anyway," answered Mom. "I've already discussed it with Ms. Brown."

---

47   They say that music scholarships are much more likely when you play an unusual instrument. Like the oboe . . . or apparently the bass fiddle.

"But you wouldn't have to buy a bass fiddle," said Mr. Bumble. "You can rent it from the school. At a discount!"

"A discount?" asked Dad.

"We won't need a discount," said Mom.

"We won't?" asked Dad.

"We are going to borrow an instrument from school," said Mom. "Isn't that right, Ms. Brown?"

Ms. Brown smiled at me. "Yes, indeed. Curious will make a great tuba player."

I was stunned. Then I smiled.

"Would you like to play the tuba, Curious?" Mom asked. Then she gave me a wink.

19

Friday, 8:31 p.m.

While the other Hilltop families sat at Bridgeman's, the McCarthys sat at their kitchen table.

While the other Hilltop students were ordering super-chocolatey-triple-scoop-banana sundaes with sprinkles, the McCarthys had ice cream, whipped cream, and cherries. But Dad surprised us with homemade hot fudge. As I dipped into the gooey, fudgy goodness, I wondered how many octaves the tuba could play.

And I wondered how Mom knew I would like the tuba.

I guess Mom's senses are pretty good.

She can taste the extra clove of garlic in Dad's special sauce.

She can see without turning her head.

She can feel if your temperature is 0.2 degrees above 98.6 degrees Fahrenheit.[48]

She can smell a dirty sock from three blocks away.

She can hear a naughty word from behind a closed door.

But I figure Mom must have a sixth sense. That is when you can figure things out with something other

---

48   Scientists use Celsius, not Fahrenheit. But Mom's not a scientist.

than your five senses. That's how she knew
that I would like the tuba. Maybe that was more
evidence for my hypothesis. Mom was pretty quiet.
Maybe that is how she heard some of my comments
about the tuba.

But with all those super-sensing abilities, I
wondered why Mom couldn't keep track of her keys.

John Glenn was laughing. "Curious will never be
able to get that tuba onto the bus!"

"Quiet down, John Glenn," said Mom. "I am going to read to you while you finish your ice cream tonight. It is getting late."

"But she will get stuck!" he laughed.

"She won't get stuck," said Mom. "We will figure something out. She is not the first kid in the world to play the tuba. Just the first McCarthy."

Mom opened the book she had picked out for the boys. She started to read *If You Ever Want to Bring a Piano to the Beach, DON'T!*[49] When she finished, John Glenn said, "Curious, if you ever want to bring your tuba to the beach, DON'T!" And he rolled onto the floor, dragging Ben and Edison with him.

"Come on, John Glenn," said Mom. "Time for bed."

She herded my little brothers up the stairs. My sisters and I trailed behind them.

After I brushed my teeth, I lay down and thought about the tuba.

---

49   This is a picture book by Elise Parsley. And as you can probably imagine, this made John Glenn crack up even more.

I hoped that Dad wouldn't try to make me a practice one out of a garden hose, a funnel, and some duct tape. Then I listened very carefully. I could hear Mom's voice from the boys' room.

". . . good you are thinking about how to deal with such a large . . ."

". . . Bumble . . ."

". . . but you are going to be nice and tall . . ."

". . . so *you* might like to play the bass fiddle . . ."

I think I even heard her giving him a big smooch. I imagined a lipstick kiss on his cheek. I smiled.

Conclusions

I heard Mom quietly close the boys' door. Then I heard the stairs creak. And then I heard her ask Dad if he had seen her keys.

Anne whispered to me, "How do you know when an alto is standing by your door?"

"I don't know. How?" I asked.

"They can't find their key, and they don't know when to come in," she answered.

I laughed. I thought about all that had happened that week. Conclusions can help scientists make sense of things. Here are my conclusions for the week:

- There are lots of different types of music. Even burping can be musical.
- Mom may lose her keys, but at least she doesn't lose her pitch.
- Scientists should leave the microphones to the musicians.

- Some people may have perfect pitch, but others are the perfect height.

And as for my hypothesis? Yes, you really do hear more when you are quiet. Just ask Mom.

SCIENCE STUNT
WHAT DOES SOUND LOOK LIKE?

This experiment will give you a closer look at sound. I mean it – you'll be able to actually see how it works!

What you need:

- empty bowl
- rubber band
- plastic wrap
- colored sugar (big crystals work best)

What you do:

1. Cover the bowl with a piece of plastic wrap.
2. Put the rubber band over the plastic and around the bowl, so that the plastic is held in place. It should be tight like a drum.
3. Sprinkle a pinch of sugar in the middle of the plastic.
4. Lower down so you are close to the bowl, and say the words *Curious McCarthy* in a loud voice. The crystals should bounce!

What is happening:

Sound is made by vibrations. The vibrations of your voice made the plastic vibrate too. If you don't believe me and think your breath made it move, try humming instead. Then experiment with different volumes and sounds. Does the sugar dance differently?

For more science stunts, visit www.torychristie.com

ᕲᕳ GLOSSARY ᕲᕳ

ability (uh-BIL-i-tee)–the power to do something

discount (DISS-kount)–reduced price

embouchure (OM-boo-shur)–the adjustment of a player's mouth to the mouthpiece of a wind instrument

evidence (EV-uh-dehnss)–information and facts that help prove something

frequency (FREE-kwuhn-see)–the number of sound waves that pass a fixed point each second

hypothesis (hye-POTH-uh-siss)–a prediction that can be tested about how a scientific investigation or experiment will turn out

inefficient (in-uh-FISH-uhnt)–wasteful of time or energy

observation (ob-zur-VAY-shuhn)–an act of gathering information by noting facts or occurances

pitch (PICH)–the highness or lowness of a musical sound

scholarship (SKOL-ur-ship)–a grant or prize that pays for you to go to college or to follow a course of study

sensor (SEN-sur)–an instrument that detects changes in heat, sound, pressure, etc., and sends the information to a controlling device; can also refer to a sense organ, including the eyes, ears, nose, taste buds, and skin

Vietnamese (vee-et-nah-MEEZ)–the official language of Vietnam, a country in Southeast Asia

vibrate (VYE-brate)–to move or cause to move back and forth or from side to side rapidly so as to produce a quivering effect or sound

FURTHER INQUIRIES

1. Do you think Curious's hypothesis is true? Why or why not?

2. How do you think Curious felt when she tried to sing "Happy Birthday" in front of her class? What details from the story tell you this?

3. What three words could you use to describe the McCarthy family and why?

RECORD YOUR FINDINGS

1. Make a Venn diagram to compare and contrast the three music teachers: Ms. Tibble, Ms. Brown, and Mr. Bumble.

2. Write a story about the first time Curious brings her tuba home from school.

3. Think about the instruments mentioned in the book. Write a paragraph sharing which one you would choose to play and why.

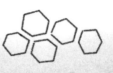

REFERENCES

Scientists should tell readers where they got their information. We call these "References." Scientists do this in case readers want to do more research.

MRS. MCCARTHY'S AND MRS. STICKLER'S REFERENCE LIST

Curious McCarthy: the Power of Observation by Tory Christie[1]

If You Ever Want to Bring a Piano to the Beach, Don't! by Elise Parsley

The Cricket in Times Square by George Selden

Frog and Toad Are Friends by Arnold Lobel

How Sensors Work by Victoria G. Christensen

Sarah, Plain and Tall by Patricia MacLachlan

Musical Instruments for the Curious Kid by Melody Piper[2]

---

1   This book contains a valuable slime recipe. But keep that to yourself.
2   I made up this book and I can do that because this is fiction.

ABOUT THE AUTHOR

Tory Christie is a real scientist by day and secretly writes children's books at night. When it is light outside, she studies rocks and water. After dark, she writes silly science stories that kids and grown-ups can laugh about. Although she grew up in a large family, her family was nothing like the McCarthys — honestly. The McCarthys are completely fictional — really. Tory Christie lives in Fargo, North Dakota, with her medium-sized family.

ABOUT THE ILLUSTRATOR

As a professional illustrator and designer, Mina Price has a particular love for book illustration and character design, or basically any project that allows her to draw interesting people in cool outfits. Mina graduated from the Maryland Institute College of Art with a BFA in Illustration. When she is not drawing, Mina can frequently be found baking things with lots of sugar or getting way too emotional over a good book.

MAKE MORE DISCOVERIES WITH CURIOUS!

FIND:

Videos & Contests
Games & Puzzles
Heroes & Villains
Authors & Illustrators

www.CAPSTONEKIDS.com

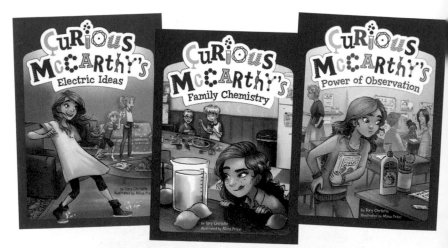

CURIOUS McCARTHY'S Electric Ideas
by Tory Christie
Illustrated by Mina Price

CURIOUS McCARTHY'S Family Chemistry
by Tory Christie
Illustrated by Mina Price

CURIOUS McCARTHY'S Power of Observation
by Tory Christie
Illustrated by Mina Price

Find cool websites and more books just like this one at
www.FACTHOUND.com. Just type in the book I.D.
9781515816430 and you're ready to go!